COME WITH ME TO
AFRICA
A PHOTOGRAPHIC JOURNEY

COME WITH ME TO
AFRICA
A PHOTOGRAPHIC JOURNEY

BY GREGORY SCOTT KREIKEMEIER

A GOLDEN BOOK • NEW YORK
Western Publishing Company, Inc.
Racine, Wisconsin 53404

Printed in Italy

4327870

DEDICATION

To Africa
—the people and the places—
and to those who pursue their dreams!

ACKNOWLEDGMENTS

In addition to a very dedicated and hardworking publishing staff and a most talented agent, I would like to thank Buddy and Lu, Ken and Joan—my parents—for giving me the opportunity and encouragement to fulfill my adventurous dreams, as crazy as they may seem.

Particular thanks to Adriaan and Alice Kraaijestein, to whom I will always be grateful and with whom I would travel anywhere! And to Youssif Basile Mousalli for exhibiting extraordinary kindness in a time of dire need.

Thanks also to the following expedition personnel who did not get mentioned in this book but whom I will always remember fondly: Ganga Seeger, Steve Baulch, Kym Sinclair, Leslie Walker—the "Aussies"; Judy Maxwell—the "Kiwi"; Monica Kaesler—the German; Chris Paul, Kathy Bergen, Leonie Meima—the "Yanks"; Paul Taylor, Joc Wheatherly, Tony, Graham and Jane Walker, Alex Alexson, Belinda Holroyd, Francis Cross—the "Brits"; Bruce Hoar, Edina Phaneuf, Craig Mclurg—the Canadians.

And finally to my good friend Patrick O'Riordan and his long-haired friend Sid for letting me crash and recover at their flat in London.

Library of Congress Catalog Card Number: 93-77647
ISBN: 0-307-15660-5/ISBN: 0-307-65660-8 (lib. bdg.)   A MCMXCIII

CONTENTS

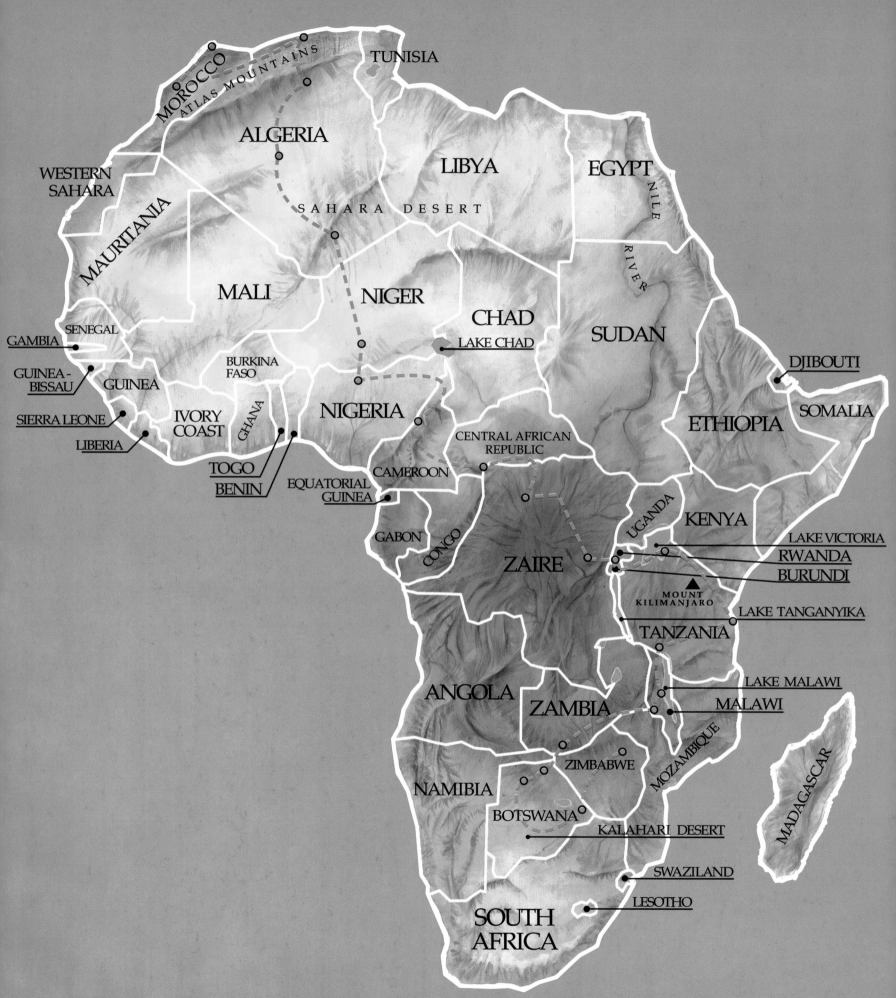

MOROCCO

ATLAS MOUNTAINS

TUNISIA

WESTERN
SAHARA

ALGERIA

LIBYA

EGYPT

MAURITANIA

SAHARA DESERT

NILE

MALI

NIGER

CHAD

SUDAN

RIVER

GAMBIA

SENEGAL

LAKE CHAD

DJIBOUTI

GUINEA-
BISSAU

BURKINA
FASO

GUINEA

SIERRA LEONE

IVORY
COAST

GHANA

NIGERIA

NIGERIA

SOMALIA

ETHIOPIA

LIBERIA

TOGO

BENIN

EQUATORIAL
GUINEA

CAMEROON

CENTRAL AFRICAN
REPUBLIC

GABON

CONGO

ZAIRE

UGANDA

KENYA

LAKE VICTORIA

RWANDA

BURUNDI

MOUNT
KILIMANJARO

LAKE TANGANYIKA

TANZANIA

ANGOLA

ZAMBIA

LAKE MALAWI

MALAWI

MOZAMBIQUE

MADAGASCAR

NAMIBIA

ZIMBABWE

BOTSWANA

KALAHARI DESERT

SWAZILAND

LESOTHO

SOUTH
AFRICA

INTRODUCTION

I had dreamed of seeing Africa from the time I was a child. It was the wild animals roaming through jungles and grasslands that I fell in love with first and wanted to see up close. As I grew older, I realized that Africa was far more than a home for elephants and lions, but I still yearned to go there.

I wanted to cross the mighty Sahara desert and feel its scorching sands beneath my feet. I wanted to get caught in a tropical storm as I trekked through rainforests. I wanted to see the mists rising from Victoria Falls. I wanted to raft down the dangerous Zambezi River and touch the great baobab trees of the Kalahari Desert. I wanted to meet the Masai tribesmen and all the other peoples of Africa.

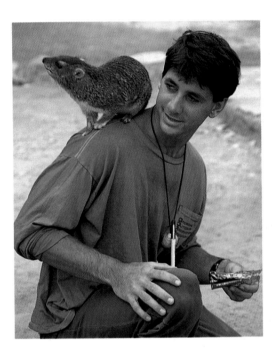

The one thing I most fervently wanted to do was to climb Mount Kilimanjaro. If ever my dream came true, I would one day stand on the snowcapped summit of Africa's highest peak.

The day came at last that I began planning what I thought of as an African photo safari. As a professional photographer and trained zoologist, I joined a multinational trans-Africa expedition that would cross almost the entire continent from north to south. There would be twelve of us, people with richly varied backgrounds, traveling together in a special expedition vehicle. Our plan was to meet in Málaga, Spain, ferry ourselves and our truck across the Mediterranean Sea to Morocco, and begin our journey.

Because Africa is huge (more than three times larger than the United States of America), we would need six months' time. We would travel through thirteen separate countries and cover more than sixteen thousand miles. We would sleep in the tents we took with us, cook many of our own meals, and buy food supplies along the way.

Our plan was to follow a route that would avoid the major cities. There are heavily populated urban and industrial areas in Africa, but we wanted to concentrate on the more remote parts of the continent. Our goals were to witness the natural beauty of the land and learn something of the culture and customs of its people. We knew this would be far easier to do if we traveled to areas that were not heavily built up or influenced by Western civilization.

We would end our trip in Zimbabwe, short of the southernmost tip of Africa, in order to avoid entering the politically troubled Republic of South Africa. We would not see "all" of Africa, but we were determined to see the best and most beautiful. An incredible journey lay ahead, and my dream of a lifetime was about to be fulfilled.

EXPEDITION VEHICLE

Our expedition vehicle was a custom-built fifteen-ton four-wheel-drive truck. It was designed to hold everything we might need and would allow us to be as self-sufficient as possible. The only supplies we would have to locate along the way were diesel fuel, food, and water. Tents, extra parts for the truck, first-aid supplies, and a fair amount of other equipment would be carried on board.

For six months our rugged truck served as home, and we became very attached to it. Because of all the stored equipment and personal gear, it wasn't roomy. Even so, it turned out to be a very reliable vehicle—and excellent protection from harsh weather of every kind.

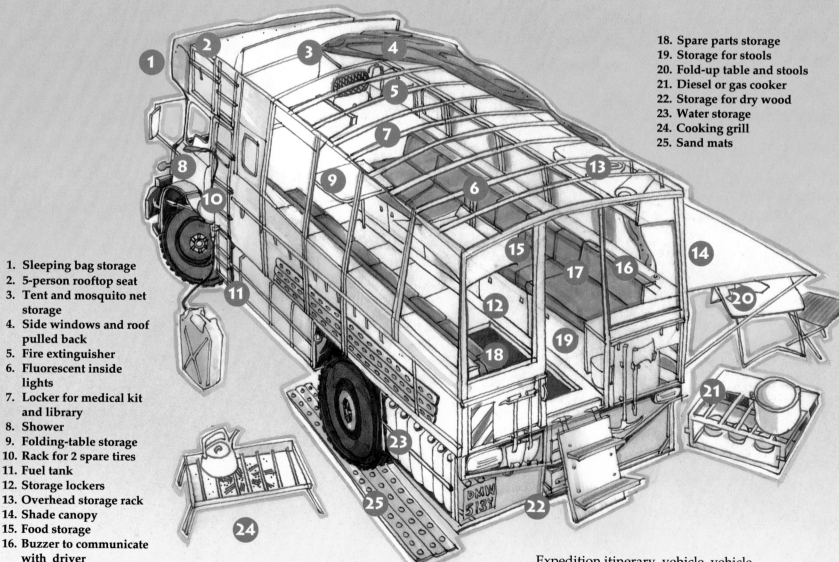

18. Spare parts storage
19. Storage for stools
20. Fold-up table and stools
21. Diesel or gas cooker
22. Storage for dry wood
23. Water storage
24. Cooking grill
25. Sand mats

1. Sleeping bag storage
2. 5-person rooftop seat
3. Tent and mosquito net storage
4. Side windows and roof pulled back
5. Fire extinguisher
6. Fluorescent inside lights
7. Locker for medical kit and library
8. Shower
9. Folding-table storage
10. Rack for 2 spare tires
11. Fuel tank
12. Storage lockers
13. Overhead storage rack
14. Shade canopy
15. Food storage
16. Buzzer to communicate with driver
17. Seats

Expedition itinerary, vehicle, vehicle equipment, and expert personnel provided by Guerba Expeditions Ltd., U.K.

WHAT TO TAKE

One of the first obstacles I had when getting ready for the trip was deciding what to take with me. Each of us was allowed a maximum of only 47 pounds of personal gear.

I planned to take 3 cameras, plus 60 batteries and more than 200 rolls of film. Along with a tripod, lenses, a flash, and 9 filters, my camera equipment alone weighed 32 pounds!

With only 15 more pounds allowed, I managed to include all of the following:

Lightweight safari pants	2 notebooks
Long-sleeved safari shirt	6 pens and pencils
2 pairs of walking shorts	Sunglasses
2 T-shirts	Binoculars
5 sets of underwear	2 African field guides
4 pairs of socks	Compass
Bush hat	Maps
Waterproof jacket	Solar-powered calculator
2 bandannas	Battery-powered razor
1 pair of sandals	2 toothbrushes
1 pair of running shoes	Tube of toothpaste
1 pair of hiking boots	2 small bars of soap
Small towel	Detergent (a little)
Washcloth	Extra shoelaces
Sleeping bag	Travel clothesline
Sheet	Flashlight
Small pillow	Water bottle
Medical kit	2 watches
Pocket-sized, solar-powered AM radio	

Believe it or not, I managed to fit all my gear into one large backpack and a small camera bag!

MOROCCO

The ferry from Spain reached port in Morocco, and our truck rolled off onto African soil. I was excited and relieved. All the months of studying maps, buying equipment, and getting permits and visas were behind us. On a sunny spring day in Morocco, our

trans-Africa expedition was beginning at last.

Morocco lies along the northwestern edge of Africa, its shoreline washed by the Atlantic Ocean. We drove down the coast to the big, bustling city of Casablanca and then turned inland.

When we reached the ancient city of Fez, we headed for its famous souk, or market. Each major city in Morocco has a souk, but the one in Fez is the largest of all—17 square miles!

The souk was crowded and noisy. Arabic craftsmen of every kind sold their wares from the tiny, cluttered shops that lined narrow, winding alleys. I walked past mountains of carpets woven with threads of every imaginable color. Polished copper bowls and brass trays glistened in the sunlight. Food merchants offered strange, exotic meats. There were cow tongues, goat heads, boiled pig tails, and sun-dried lizard meat.

Over the hubbub of the souk, I could hear a Muslim call to prayer from the nearby mosque, or place of worship. The sounds and sights of North Africa were more wonderful than I could have imagined.

In the souk in Fez, one shop offered nothing but beautiful leather shoes. Each pair was decorated with silk threads, and no two pairs were alike.

I felt I could see all of Morocco standing on this hilltop overlooking Fez.

10

Another of my favorite places in Morocco was the ruined city of Volubilis. About two thousand years ago, Roman soldiers conquered most of North Africa, including what is now known as Morocco. One of the most impressive cities the Romans built was Volubilis.

The excavated ruins stand on a high hill overlooking green, fertile valleys. Most of the buildings have fallen down over the centuries, but a number of stone walls and archways still stand.

The once-great city was deserted and quiet as I walked around. Then the sky began to darken. A storm approached, and thunder echoed through the ruins. In my mind the thunder sounded like the heavy marching of a legion of Roman soldiers long ago.

Right: Thirty-foot-high columns still stand watch over the ancient city of Volubilis, as Roman soldiers did many hundreds of years ago.

As we traveled through the Moroccan countryside, rainbows were a common sight.

As our trek across Morocco continued, we saw the snow-covered peaks of the beautiful Atlas Mountains ahead. Mount Toubkal, in the High Atlas range, is the tallest mountain in North Africa (13,671 feet). I knew it was a popular mountain to climb, and I was eager to give it a try.

My travel companions and I hired a guide named Mohammed for the climb. The trip would take three days. At first there were green, terraced hillsides and fast-flowing streams. Higher on the mountain, plant growth was sparse. We struggled up to the snow line and finally reached the summit.

The view was incredible. On the far side of the mountain, I could see the Sahara desert stretching to the horizon. In spite of the snow on the summit, bright sunshine warmed the air. However, six-hour hiking days had taken a toll on our group. Only three of us made it to the top.

On the first night of the climb, we stayed in our guide's mountainside home. Mohammed treated us to a fine meal of fresh, steaming vegetables, served with a traditional side dish of cooked grains called couscous.

In the midst of our climb up Mount Toubkal, I could look back and see the lush valley below and snowcapped mountains in the background.

The melting snow from Mount Toubkal drains to the valley below and creates beautiful waterfalls. We camped near the Cascades d'Ouzoud, and I spent one entire day exploring the area. It was a hot day, so I was happy to reach the cool falls. The sight from the bottom was magnificent. The water roared toward me with an incredible force. It created a strong wind that blew a heavy mist all around me. I was soaked and very refreshed.

After a day of adventuring, two of my fellow travelers, Adriaan and Alice Kraijestein, often cooked supper for everyone. They both enjoyed cooking and were talented at creating delicious meals from the unusual kinds of food we bought at local markets.

I, on the other hand, was an enthusiastic eater but not a natural chef. Instead, I became expert at starting up and tending the cooking fire.

Left: Before my friends Adriaan and Alice could cook supper, the food containers, table, stove, and other supplies had to be taken out of the truck and set up.

The waterfall known as the Cascades d'Ouzoud is four hundred feet high. The water plummets down into a large pond at the bottom, where people swim.

Left: Near the waterfall I met a local boy named Amil—and his donkey. Amil and his friends became my guides for the day.

13

ALGERIA

The waterfalls and green valleys disappeared when we crossed into Algeria and headed south. Algeria is Africa's second-largest country, and most of it is covered by the great Sahara desert.

The Sahara is the largest, hottest desert on earth. In size it is about as big as the United States. Water is scarce in the desert, so we had to begin to limit our use. Drinking too little water in the heat is dangerous and causes dehydration, so there was no limit on drinking water. However, for all other purposes, such as sponge baths, each of us was limited to one cup a day.

In areas of the Sahara where there was no paved road, we often bogged down in soft sand.

Sand dunes often appeared in the middle of the roads, forcing us to drive off onto the desert sands to get around them.

As the sandstorm approached, blowing sand began to cover the road. Shortly after this photo was taken, the road disappeared completely.

Paved roads are scarce in the desert. Much of the way there were none, and we were forced to navigate by compass. Driving on sand, the truck often lost traction and came to a halt. Luckily, the sand mats we carried with us worked well. We would get out of the truck, shove the mats under the wheels, and push the truck with all our might. Sooner or later, we were always able to get it moving again.

During the day, temperatures were over 100° F. The sand was unbearably hot. We had to keep our shoes on so we wouldn't burn our feet. The metal parts of the truck also grew extremely hot, and we had to be careful not to burn ourselves.

At the end of the first week in the desert, a powerful sandstorm hit us. The sky grew black as coal, and the wind was so strong I could barely stand up. The wind was dangerous because it carried tons of sand grains. Any exposed areas of skin could be sandblasted raw. To prevent this, I wore a hat, a scarf, and as many kinds of protective clothing as I could. The wind-blown dust was so thick I had to wear a bandanna over my mouth and nose, just to be able to breathe. My eyes burned from the sand and dust that managed to get inside my goggles.

The sandstorm blew hour after hour. Late in the day we tried to set up our tents, but the wind ripped them from the ground. I finally managed to secure my tent with forty-two extra tent stakes and sixty feet of rope.

Inside the tent that night, I witnessed an amazing event. Wind-blown sand grains were hitting the outside of the tent with such force that the tent became electrically charged. I huddled inside and watched as tiny bolts of lightning jumped from the walls of the tent to the aluminum center poles. Luckily, the electricity wasn't strong enough to do me any harm.

The storm lasted for two days. By the time it was over, the landscape had changed completely. Entire sand dunes were gone, and new ones had appeared. The truck was half-buried in sand and dust. It took us several hours to dig out and finally continue on our way.

After the storm, it was no surprise to me to discover that few people live in the Sahara. Attempts to live there have usually ended in failure. Algeria was once a French colony, and we came upon one of the old French fortresses. Fort Mirabel was a training center for the French Foreign Legion. In the end the soldiers abandoned the fort. Little by little, it is being buried by desert sand.

Over fifty years ago, Fort Mirabel was an important link in the chain of French fortresses across Algeria. It now lies in ruins.

The Hoggar Mountains are unique in the way they rise up suddenly from the floor of the desert.

Five more long days of driving across flat, barren desert brought us to the beautiful and ragged Hoggar Mountains. Stretching across the southern part of Algeria, the mountains are actually giant pillars of rock several hundred feet high. They rise out of nowhere in the middle of the desert and are a welcome relief to desert travelers. They are especially magnificent to see at sundown. Sand grains blowing in the air around the mountains help create brilliant red and gold sunsets.

I hired a small off-road vehicle for two days to drive through the mountains and photograph this handsome area.

I met Tari in a small Algerian village. The young girl told me that she could not go to school because she had no ink pens. She was very happy when I gave her several pens. In return she offered me two loaves of freshly baked bread.

17

NIGER

We reached the Algerian border and crossed into Niger, still deep in the Sahara. Like Algeria, Niger is a former French colony. Also like Algeria, the country is in great part covered by desert.

Driving through the Sahara, I began to realize that most of it is not made up of loose, blowing sand and dunes. In fact, only about 10 percent of the Sahara is covered with dunes. The rest is flat, barren earth dotted with occasional rock outcroppings.

Even in the most desolate parts of the desert, there are some animals. During the day, I would occasionally see a lizard or spider scurrying across the hot sand. However, desert animals are more likely to come out of hiding at night, when the temperature drops to as low as 50° F.

Camping on sand dunes is very enjoyable. The sand is as flat and soft as a mattress.

When we first entered the desert, I slept out in the open at night. However, a large scorpion crawled into my sleeping bag late one evening. After that I slept in a tent!

The best way to put up a tent on the desert is to scrape away the hot surface layer of sand and set up the tent on the cooler sand beneath. I also learned to pile sand up under the tent floor to use as a pillow. As it turned out, the desert was very comfortable at night.

Blowing desert winds constantly change the shapes of the sand dunes.

It was a relief to leave the harshest part of the desert behind and see grass and brush growing.

The desert is also beautiful at night. The sky is clear as glass, and there are millions upon millions of stars. They blanket the sky from horizon to horizon, glowing like sparks from an open campfire. The stars are so bright that I was able to write my journal entries by their light.

Driving south by day, we finally reached the southern edge of the desert and entered into the semidesert scrub region known as the Sahel. In this low-lying area we finally began to see small trees and bushes again.

We also began to meet people again, mostly nomadic herdsmen and their families. The nomads raise goats, camels, and donkeys and lead their animals to graze in various parts of the land. Water is scarce on the surface but abundant underground. Deep wells are dug, some more than three hundred feet down. The local herdsmen spend hours each day just drawing water from the wells.

To reach the water, the people lower large animal-skin bags into the well. Long ropes are attached to the bags. When the water bags are full, the ropes are attached to donkeys or camels. The animals are led away from the well, pulling the water to the surface. The herdsmen pour the water out into large clay containers. From these troughs people can fill their individual water jugs.

We spent many hours at desert wells, filling our own water containers. I enjoyed it every time because there was always a crowd of interesting people to talk to at the wells, along with herds of noisy animals to admire.

Right: In a local market in Niger, I saw camels being bought and sold. Camels are still used for transportation. They are also a valuable source of meat and leather.

Life in the desert centers around the wells, where water is drawn every day from sunup to sundown.

NIGERIA

Once we entered our fourth country, Nigeria, I began to notice the land changing from hot and dry desert conditions in the north to hot and humid tropical conditions in the south. Much of the land is farmed. Other stretches are overgrown with green, grassy meadows. We discovered that water was easier to find. The sun still shone brightly, and the air was hot, but it was not nearly as hot as it had been in the desert. The population was changing, too, from the lighter-skinned Arab people we had met in Morocco and Algeria to darker-skinned African people.

Nigeria is Africa's most populous country. No matter where we went, we saw people. Hundreds of friendly, curious visitors came to our nightly campsites.

This colorful male agama lizard patrolled a wall next to our campsite.

Although these children had no desks, chairs, or electricity in their classroom, they felt lucky to be in school.

Below: Unlike the cramped indoor souks of Morocco, Nigerian markets are set up in open fields. The people in the countryside are relatively poor, and they did not offer a wide variety of fruits and vegetables in the marketplace.

Left: Having just spent four weeks crossing the flat, sandy desert, I was relieved to see rolling green meadows and hills again.

CAMEROON

From Nigeria we crossed the border into northern Cameroon. As we drove into small villages along the way, friendly groups of villagers would come out to meet us and welcome us to their country. Unfortunately, we couldn't speak each other's languages, but we communicated as well as possible with simple hand gestures.

Overpopulation has created food shortages in some parts of Cameroon, and for the first time I noticed children suffering from malnutrition. The northern part of the country doesn't receive much rainfall, and crops grow poorly. As we headed south, however, we found a more tropical climate. Food and water were more abundant, and the people were generally healthier.

The people in Cameroon were particularly friendly. As we drove toward one of the first villages on our route, this group of residents came out to wave and say hello.

Right: I was amazed at how easily these women balanced the heavy weight they were carrying. The path was steep and uneven, but the women kept a quick pace.

In the north a chain of volcanic mountains runs from the coastline on the South Atlantic Ocean inland along the border with Nigeria. Part of the stretch of mountains includes a beautiful area called Roumsiki. In this cool mountain setting, three-hundred-foot volcanic-rock spires encircle a hidden green valley.

Not yet aware of the protected valley, I approached Roumsiki from the outside and climbed to the top of one of the rock spires. The view below was breathtaking. A tiny village was nestled in a wide, soft carpet of green. The valley was a mass of thick grass, nourished by daily rain showers.

As I walked the trail leading down into the valley, two women carrying heavy loads on their heads passed me. They were walking down the rocky trail faster than I was, but they were able to turn, say hello, and continue on without once losing their balance.

At the bottom of the trail, I came to the small village or group of huts I had seen from the top.

Confident of their bracelet-making skills, these boys offered to teach me the process.

Walking into the village, I was soon surrounded by five young boys. I admired the bracelets they were making, which I soon learned are created out of the fibrous roots of a local plant. The boys were eager to show me how they first chewed the plant roots to soften them and then pulled out long stringy fibers. They twisted the fibers together to form rope and finally braided the rope strands together into bracelets.

Another boy in the village wanted to show me his pet lamb. He was responsible for raising the lamb and keeping it out of trouble. However, the lamb's mother didn't seem to think the boy's plan was a good one. She bleated noisily and bit the boy's shorts again and again.

Right: I have never seen a child as proud of a pet as this boy was of his lamb.

In a nearby village in northern Cameroon, I met an interesting man known locally as the Crab Sorcerer. He was very outgoing and spoke some English and French, as well as several local languages. He was well known and respected throughout the area because of his ability to predict the future.

I was invited to visit the man in his small hut and was fortunate enough to be treated to a sample of his talent. He is called the Crab Sorcerer because he works his magic with the help of a large land crab. The man sat me in the middle of the hut next to a low fire of smoking embers. First he tossed a handful of shells, beans, stones, and small bones on the ground. Then he reached into a large clay pot and brought out the crab. He waved the crab through the smoke and then placed it on the ground in the middle of the various objects. The crab immediately grabbed two beans from the ground. Luckily for me, the sorcerer interpreted this as a sign that the rest of the expedition would be successful and full of adventure.

The Crab Sorcerer displayed his skills inside the hut at the far right but would not allow me to take photographs. The middle hut was the one in which he lived. The largest hut belonged to relatives.

CENTRAL AFRICAN REPUBLIC

From Cameroon we headed east into the Central African Republic. We were in the southern half of the country, where it is hot, humid, and very tropical. We were also near the equator, which is an imaginary line drawn

around the middle of the world, marking an equal distance to the North and South poles. At the equator it rains part of each day.

We were often surrounded by dense jungle. At night the jungle would come alive with the eerie hoots and roars of animals I couldn't see. Hordes of insects, too, chirped in a nightly chorus around the camp.

The noise was sometimes so loud, we could barely hear one another. Large swarms of hungry mosquitoes often invaded the camp at night, attracted by the bright lights in the truck and the smell of humans.

The roads we traveled during the day were not paved. When it rained, they turned into mud bogs. There were large potholes everywhere, and our progress was slow.

As we drove toward the capital city of Bangui one morning, we rounded a sharp curve and put on the brakes. On the narrow bridge ahead, an overloaded truck with a broken axle had come to a stop. There was no room to pass. Luckily, the stream beneath the bridge wasn't deep. We dragged out the sand mats and were able to get the truck across the stream and around the broken-down vehicle.

A thick cloud of mosquitoes managed to get inside the truck at night. Mosquitoes in this area carried the dangerous disease malaria, so we soaked ourselves and our clothes in bug repellent to keep them from biting.

When we were caught behind a disabled vehicle that was stuck on a bridge, I thought we would be delayed for hours. Luckily, our sand mats helped us create a path across the water.

The bush country we were traveling through was dotted with small traditional villages. I was fascinated by the village huts and wanted to see how they were constructed. I visited several and discovered that the walls of many are made of dried-mud bricks supported by an internal wooden frame. The roof of each hut is also held up by a wood frame, which is then covered with several thick layers of grass. When it rains, the huts are completely waterproof. On hot days, they stay cool inside. During cool nights, they are warm.

Small villages were a common sight along roads in the Central African Republic.

Some huts had no mud-brick walls and were constructed entirely of grass instead. Large bundles were strapped together for walls, and the bunched roof grasses came all the way down to the ground.

When we reached the city of Bangui, we parked at the town campsite, next to a large outdoor market. Bangui is a poor city with a high unemployment rate. Robbery was common at the campsite, so two of us guarded the truck at all times during the five days we were there.

At the market we were able to buy a good two-week supply of fruits and vegetables: bananas, pineapples, corn, potatoes, onions, and more. During our time in Bangui, we were also able to tune up the truck—and just relax, which we didn't often do. Thankfully, there were no encounters with thieves.

The village huts were dark inside but very clean. There was little furniture. The people who lived there slept on goatskins and used small wooden neck rests as pillows. In some huts I saw a small cooking fire and a few clay pots for storing food and water.

Adriaan and Alice took a turn guarding the truck at the Bangui town campsite.

The roads in Zaire were the worst of any. The loosely packed dirt on this road suddenly gave way, and our truck almost rolled over in an accident that could have ended the expedition.

ZAIRE

I was happy when we crossed the border into Zaire. Zaire is a large country at the heart of the tropics, rich with lush jungles, flowing rivers, and high mountains. Zaire is the home of the Bantu and Pygmy peoples.

In Zaire we finally crossed the equator, which meant that we had traveled down half the continent. The rest of the expedition would take place in the Southern Hemisphere.

The eastern edge of Zaire borders on an area of high volcanic mountains covered with thick rainforests. This is where the world-famous lowland gorillas live. Adriaan, Alice, and I trekked through the mountain region of Kahuzi-Biega in search of these magnificent giants.

The jungle was amazingly dense with growth. To make a path for us, our guide slashed through the undergrowth with his machete—a large, heavy knife. We climbed a small hill, and suddenly, not twenty feet away, we saw a group of seven gorillas sitting quietly in a small clearing, feeding on grass and leaves. They were absolutely huge animals, with large, powerful limbs and thick coats of black and gray hair. I could smell their musty aroma in the humid air. When the click of my camera finally scared them away, I was heartbroken.

Rainforests provide the perfect climate for exquisite tropical flowers.

Above and right: In order to get close to the shy lowland gorillas, we inched our way slowly and quietly up the mountain.

BURUNDI

We crossed the eastern border of Zaire into Burundi, one of Africa's smallest countries. It is a beautiful mountainous nation with fertile farmlands, including huge coffee plantations. To create more space for planting, farmers are constantly cutting down Burundi's forests. The cleared trees and bushes are then burned. Wherever we went, I could see the smoke of several fires in the distance. The fires spew an enormous amount of ash and soot into the air, creating a constant smog in some areas. I hope the people will someday realize what they're doing to the air and decide to reduce the burning.

The mighty Nile River, the largest in the world, winds its way north for over four thousand miles through eastern Africa to Egypt, where it finally empties into the Mediterranean Sea. The southernmost source of this famed river is said to be a small spring high atop one of Burundi's mountains. Visiting the sight, I found it hard to believe that the ancient river of the pharaohs could begin with such a tiny trickle.

Small waterfalls are common in Burundi, as water runs off the many mountains. My favorite waterfall was Karera Falls. We set up camp at the base of the falls on a hot night. The falling mist cooled the air, and the noise of the roaring water lulled me to sleep.

The sunsets in Burundi were always very colorful. Unfortunately, the color is the result of air pollution.

This small spring is considered by many to be the southernmost source of the Nile.

Right: During the night, the flow of water at Karera Falls increased because of rain in the mountains. We set up camp in a dry area at the bottom of the falls, but when I awoke in the morning, my tent and equipment were soaking wet.

Lake Tanganyika runs along the western border of Burundi. The lake, 420 miles long, is the longest freshwater lake in the world. We camped on the beach for two days—and grabbed the chance, among other things, to do some much-needed laundry.

Lake Tanganyika is a vast inland sea. It even has large waves breaking along the sandy white shoreline. The waves and beaches made me think I was at the edge of an ocean. However, the water in the lake is not salty.

We camped on this beach at Lake Tanganyika.

The Burundi markets overflow with energy. People travel long distances to buy or sell their goods. The market is also a major means of relaying news and staying in touch with friends.

Burundi is one of the most densely populated countries in the world, and the crowded markets were fascinating. There were people everywhere, dressed in particularly colorful clothes. Everyone was interested in our truck, and a huge crowd surrounded us when we stopped at the marketplace. The children loved to climb up the truck's side ladders and jump down from the top into the soft dirt.

Left: We found this shaky observation tower in a small national park along the lakeshore. From the top, I used my binoculars and saw half-submerged hippos in the distance. Seeing the hippos was exciting because it meant that we were entering the major game park area of Africa.

TANZANIA

Leaving the mountains and forests of Burundi behind, we crossed the border into Tanzania and ferried across Lake Victoria to the plains of East

Africa. The wild animals I dreamed of as a child are the main reason that most people visit Africa, and no African country is more famous for its animals than Tanzania.

Land development and poaching have forced many African governments to protect their animals inside national game parks. Some of the parks are small. Others are thousands of square miles in size. Tanzania contains two of the world's most famous game parks: the Serengeti National Park and the Ngorongoro Crater Conservation Area.

I was thrilled to be standing at the entrance gate of one of Tanzania's most important game parks.

I couldn't believe my luck when I spotted this giraffe family standing in a neat line.

These lions tried to ambush a wildebeest near our truck, but the hunted animal outran the lions and got away.

Seeing animals in the wild was everything I had ever imagined. The first large creatures I saw in the Serengeti National Park were giraffes. From a distance their brown-blotched coloring blended in so well with the savanna, or plains, around them that they were hard to see. Until I saw one closer, I did not realize how large these animals are. As we sat in our truck one morning, an eighteen-foot male giraffe walked toward us and actually stepped over the front of the truck.

Everyone who goes to the Serengeti wants to see lions. Lions live in large family groups called prides. They feed at night and spend their days mostly sleeping and resting in the shade. However, I saw lions awake during the day on several occasions, hiding in the tall grass. As we sat close to our campfire at night, I often heard the low, grumbling roars of lions speaking to one another in the distance. One night three large females decided to visit our camp. They casually walked past the tents, snarled and grunted, then disappeared into the darkness.

The cheetah is the only cat with claws that do not retract. The claws provide excellent traction, allowing the animals to run at very high speeds.

The next morning I saw a lioness asleep in the grass at the side of a road. The truck rolled to a stop, and I got out to take her photograph. She was very close. Too close, in fact. At that distance she could easily have reached out with her plate-sized paw and grabbed me. Luckily, her belly was full, and she was content to sleep.

Another plains predator that I was fortunate enough to see was the cheetah. Cheetahs are much smaller than lions and do not live in family groups. As I watched a herd of zebras on the distant plain one morning, I noticed movement in a clump of grass only yards away. Suddenly two fully grown cheetahs stood up. Their spotted coats had been excellent camouflage. If the animals hadn't stood up, I never would have seen them at all.

I hoped to see the cheetahs run because they are the fastest of all land animals. From a stand-still, they can reach a speed of sixty miles an hour in three seconds. However, the two cheetahs in front of me walked away slowly on long, slender legs. Their powerful shoulders rocked back and forth gracefully with every step.

Left: The head of this lioness was as large as a basketball, and her face showed the scars of past battles. She was beautiful and powerful, the largest and most feared predator in all of Africa.

Ostriches are the largest birds in the world and cannot fly. During my encounter with this male ostrich, I wasn't sure *who* was more startled!

I watched this beautiful gray-headed kingfisher dive into a nearby pond and capture small fish.

The strangest and least graceful animal I saw in the Serengeti was an ostrich. While eating lunch one day, I heard a noise behind some tall rocks. I walked quietly around the rocks—and stopped. There, towering eight feet in the air and staring down at me, was the ugliest bird I had ever seen. I jumped back. The ostrich let out a loud snort, raised its eyebrows, and ran off as fast as it could go. It was a funny sight—a giant ball of legs and feathers thundering away through the grass.

Throughout the park hippopotamuses lounge each day in what are called hippo pools. I spent many hours watching the animals in these pools, amazed at how perfectly they are adapted to life in the water. A hippo's ears, eyes, and nostrils are located on the top of its head, so the animal can hear, see, and breathe, even when most of its body is underwater, staying cool and moist. At night hippos leave the water to feed on grass. They have incredibly large appetites and may eat more than fifty pounds of grass at a feeding.

Hippos look peaceful, but each year they kill more people in Africa than any other kind of animal.

Hippos have bad tempers and can be aggressive. I tried to get close to one, but found myself running back to the truck every time. I didn't want to be chased by an angry four-ton hippo!

43

This was the view from our campsite, looking down into the Ngorongoro Crater. The crater lake is in the distance.

The Serengeti shares its southern border with another famous conservation area known as the Ngorongoro Crater. The crater is actually an enormous extinct volcano. Large numbers of animals live on a vast plain inside the crater. It is the second-largest crater in the world.

A wide, shallow lake covers the center of the crater plain. Because of minerals in the crater, the water is very salty. Most animals avoid the lake, preferring to drink from small, spring-fed, freshwater ponds instead.

From the rim of the crater, the lake far below seemed to be covered with pink spots. As we made the steep drive down to the crater floor, I realized that the spots on the water were actually thousands of flamingos. The pink birds feed on tiny crablike animals that live in the salty lake.

On the crater plain, you can see many species of game, large and small. There are herds of wildebeests, elephants, and zebras, living side by side.

44

The brightly colored coats of these African wild dog pups help them identify one another.

Zebras and flamingos enjoying the crater lake together.

Large herds of wildebeests roam the crater floor.

The flamingos' beautiful color comes from the food they eat.

This curious vervet monkey studied its reflection in my camera lens.

Left: Vervet monkeys were a common sight in the crater park.

The Masai people have been cattle herders for many hundreds of years, but recently they have been forced to share their traditional lands with conservation areas.

I was sorry to leave the Serengeti behind, but I was very excited about our next destination: Mount Kilimanjaro, near the Kenyan border. The famous mountain that I so much wanted to climb is a not-fully-extinct volcano, 19,340 feet high. Covered with glaciers year round, it is the world's highest free-standing mountain.

Thousands of people try to climb the mountain every year, but only about one-third make it to the top. I joined a group of six climbers. Together we hired a local guide named George, as well as porters to help carry our gear. The climb would take four days. At night we would sleep in wooden huts maintained by the Mount Kilimanjaro National Park.

On the second day of the climb, I took out a small kite I had been carrying in a plastic tube. I had brought the kite with me to fly it from the top of the mountain, but first it needed a test

We slept in these mountainside huts. In the background is the snowy summit of Mount Kilimanjaro.

flight. George, our guide, was not happy to see the kite. Once we made the dangerous trip to the peak, he did not want any delays.

At the start of the fourth day, we began our climb at 1 A.M. We wanted to reach the summit by early morning, before clouds closed in around the peak for the day.

On the first day of the climb, we trekked through thick tropical rainforests that surround the base of the mountain.

It was a grueling seven-hour hike up icy slopes. The frigid temperature was -10°F., and the wind blew with gale force. In the end only two of us made it to the top, plus George. We reached the summit just as the sun began to warm the mountain.

The view was beyond description. It seemed as though all of Africa lay at our feet. I was giddy with happiness. My hands were nearly frozen, but I managed to pull out the kite. After a couple of nosedives, the kite finally flew in the wild wind. By this time, George's mood had changed. As the small rainbow-colored kite rose in the cold air, George smiled and cheered.

The final part of the climb was agony. Because of the altitude, the air was very thin. My lungs ached with every breath.

As far as I know, my kite is the first and only to have flown from the top of Mount Kilimanjaro.

MALAWI

We made a quick trip to the coast of Tanzania, on the Indian Ocean, then headed southwest to a small sliver of a country called Malawi. Almost 20 percent of Malawi is covered by Lake Malawi, which is another of the largest freshwater lakes in the world. Most of the people living around the lake are fishermen. They spend each day out on the water, catching their fish with nets and long, hand-held lines.

One morning Adriaan, Alice, and I talked one of the fishermen into paddling us out onto the lake in his handmade wooden boat for a trip to Bird Island. The island is tiny, inhabited by ferocious-looking monitor lizards and large

Fishermen clean their nets after a successful day's fishing on Lake Malawi.

colonies of nesting cormorants. All the rocks and bushes on the island were white with bird droppings, and the smell was terrible.

As expected, there were birds everywhere. They squawked and dive-bombed as we walked around the island.

On the trip back to shore, the wind picked up. Our guide hoisted a sail he had made out of plastic trash bags. The sail worked, and we made good time.

When we left peaceful Lake Malawi, we headed west for the capital city of Lilongwe, in order to stock up on supplies. Then we crossed the border and entered Zambia, our eleventh country.

This ingenious fisherman had constructed a sail out of old plastic trash bags.

These cormorants were sunning themselves on Bird Island.

ZAMBIA

Once in Zambia we drove across vast open plains, large cultivated fields, and grass-lands fenced for cattle. At one time the British colony of Northern Rhodesia, Zambia is a country plagued with debt and political unrest. This is true of a number of African nations. However, Zambia is tranquil on the surface at least, stretching out across a gently rolling plateau.

The greatest sight in Zambia—and one of the great natural wonders of the world—is Victoria Falls. The first European to discover the falls was David Livingstone, a famous nineteenth-century missionary and explorer. The falls were named in honor of Queen Victoria of England.

The waterfall is huge. We were still six miles away when I first saw its mist rising in the sky. The constant blowing mist has even created a small rainforest near the falls.

To see the falls from the air, I went for a breathtaking plane ride. The pilot flew so low and close to the falls that we were surrounded by mist.

Below: Sunlight shining through the mist from Victoria Falls created rainbows everywhere I looked.

Left: Victoria Falls is actually made up of ten different waterfalls that come together in the same gorge. The tallest is as high as a thirty-story building.

53

White-water rafting on the Zambezi was more than we bargained for. After flipping over, we floated on the upside-down raft and took a breather.

The powerful Zambezi River supplies the water for Victoria Falls. At its widest the Zambezi measures more than a mile across; there the river suddenly drops into a deep and narrow chasm. At this point it becomes one of the best rivers in the world for white-water rafting.

Alice, Adriaan, and I joined three others and went for a wet and wild rafting trip down the river. Our guide controlled the raft with large oars. He did a good job until we went over a particularly fast rapid and slammed headfirst into a monstrous wave—a twenty-foot-high wall of water. The wave tossed the raft in the air like a toy boat and flipped it over. We managed to climb onto the capsized raft and float through the next rapids. When we hit calmer waters, we turned the raft over and climbed back inside.

One stretch of rapids was too dangerous to run. We carried the raft past it and then continued down the river.

One night we were invited to a celebration at a Zambian village not far from our campsite. The performances were stunning. Four male drummers and a group of seven women began the festivities by beating drums and clapping blocks together. Several women with strong, beautiful voices sang while four dancers began moving to a very fast rhythm. The dancers wore boldly colored costumes and frightening masks. Later they were joined by a dancer who performed on ten-foot-high stilts.

The evening was spectacular and lasted for several hours. By the time it was over, I was exhausted—and I hadn't even participated!

Top: The colorfully dressed women created wonderful dance rhythms with nothing but drums and blocks.

Middle: The costumed dancers moved in a syncopated rhythm with the music.

Bottom: A line of male drummers changed the dance tempo by beating on very large drums.

Left: The stilt walker was a dancer with incredible balance. He was able to hop on one stilt and even jumped completely off the ground several times.

BOTSWANA

We headed south into Botswana. This would be as far south as we could travel without

entering South Africa, a country we had agreed to avoid. Unlike Zambia, most of Botswana is covered by semidesert and scrubland—inhabited by groups of nomadic San Bushmen. There are several game parks in Botswana, including Chobe National Park, famous for its immense herds of elephants.

The roads in Chobe Park are in such terrible condition that many tourists stay away. As a result, we had the elephants all to ourselves, which was wonderful. The animals were most impressive in the evenings, when they would gather in large herds around the watering holes. There was a funny game that the young

Elephants are extremely interesting animals. I never grew tired of watching them.

elephants liked to play. First they would wade into the deep part of the pool, leaving only the tips of their trunks above water. Suddenly the young animals would splash their way out of the water back to their mothers, trumpeting wildly. The adult elephants always kept an eye on us as we watched the babies play.

Elephants cool off by bathing in muddy water. Out of the water, the mud dries and protects their skin from the sun.

Local guides poled us through the swamp in dugout canoes called makurus.

We left Chobe and drove to the delta of the Okavango River. The delta is actually a swamp, the largest in the world, and home to thousands of different kinds of plants and animals. We took a long boat trip deep into the swamp and then set up camp on a small island.

Being in the heart of the swamp was fantastic. I have never seen so many species of birds in one area. Groups of large animals, such as elephants, zebras, hippos, and buffalo, also live in the swamp, moving from island to island to feed.

The water was clean and clear. Insects were few. The Okavango swamp turned out to be one of my all-time favorite places to camp and see wildlife.

The fish eagle that lives in the swamp is related to the American bald eagle.

Small crocodiles liked to visit our camp and feed on scraps of our food.

Palm-tree islands dot the swamp. Rings of colored grasses grow outward from their shores.

Before leaving the Okavango Delta, I was able to find a pilot with a small airplane who showed me the massive swamp from the air. From above I could see that much of the water in the swamp is covered with layers of bright green lily pads. Crisscrossing the lily pads were veins of blue water where animals had traveled. Large clumps of palm trees were everywhere. Smaller islands of brightly colored grasses surrounded them like drops of rainbow-colored oil on a calm pond.

The shadow of our plane disturbed the birds. As we flew over, huge flocks of them rose from the marsh.

Sundown in the swamp was a peaceful, quiet time.

Our truck bogged down in a salt pan, one of the unstable salty clay areas of the Kalahari Desert. After digging from dawn to dusk for two days and almost running out of water, we finally managed to free the vehicle.

Beyond the delta and leading far to the south is the Kalahari Desert. Unlike the Sahara in the north, the Kalahari has no soft dunes and is mostly flat and barren.

The Kalahari is famous for its gigantic baobab trees. Some of the trees are two thousand years old and measure more than sixty-five feet around. (Your waist might be twenty-five *inches* around!) The trunks of the trees are hollow and collect water. The majestic trees are considered sacred and are never cut down.

Camping under a giant baobab is a strange and wonderful experience. At night the desert winds blow through the ancient branches, and the great sprawling limbs crack and moan eerily through the night.

Baobab trees are huge. Our truck was parked behind the tree in front and is completely hidden from view.

ZIMBABWE

One hundred and sixty-five wonderful days had passed since we began our expedition. Sadly enough, we were entering our last country, Zimbabwe. We planned to leave Africa when we got to the capital, Harare.

Once in Zimbabwe, we drove to the Rhodes Matopos National Park, famous for its rare white rhinos. The rhinos are not white, in fact, but gray. Their name is a mistranslation of the local name, which means "wide," not "white," and refers to their mouths, not their color.

I couldn't believe my good fortune early one afternoon in the park when I saw five white rhinos feeding together. Rhinos can be aggressive and dangerous. They can also run as fast as thirty miles an hour, so I stayed a safe distance away.

There are many small caves in the park with ancient wall paintings created by San Bushmen four thousand years ago. The paint used was a mixture of crushed rocks, plants, and the blood of animals.

Some of the wind-sculpted granite boulders in Rhodes Matopos National Park are as big as a school bus.

I would have been happy to see just one white rhino. When I saw five together, I was thrilled beyond belief.

On our way to Harare, we also visited the Great Zimbabwe ruins, the remains of a large ancient city. The impressive ruins are silent proof of the advanced level of civilization reached by the people who lived in this area long before European colonists arrived.

The ruins are a mass of crumbling walls and collapsed roofs. Part of the fortified city was carved out of an immense rock hill. The only way to enter was to climb a narrow, steep set of stairs chiseled directly into the rock.

The doorways were long and narrow because the stone walls were five feet thick.

Baboons are common in this part of Africa. They invaded our campsite and carried off food and shiny utensils.

Great Zimbabwe ruins are the remains of a once-great city of eighteen thousand people.

These dancers were very animated and jumped high off the ground.

This beautiful girl chanted and sang while the dancers whirled around her.

Before actually driving into Harare, we stopped in a small village outside town. As always, the villagers were friendly. When they heard that our journey was almost at an end, they decided to perform a special farewell dance for us.

The Zimbabwe villagers danced and sang with tremendous energy. I even joined in, knowing that as long as I participated, they would keep dancing. I wanted to dance and sing for another six months. I wanted the journey to go on and on. But I knew we had reached our goal. It was time to go home and plan another adventure, another dream.

EPILOGUE

From Harare I boarded a 747 jet for a ten-hour flight to London, England. That flight turned out to be the saddest of my life. I remember telling myself that I should have been happy. After all, I was clean for the first time in months. The food on the flight was excellent, and the seats were comfortable. But it was no use. All I could think about were the friendships I had formed and the incredible adventures we had shared.

I'm still sad when I remember back. Gone are the long days of sitting in the back of a dirty truck, bouncing down a rough, dusty road. There will be no more mosquito bites. No more rainstorms to soak me to the bone. No more encounters with rhinos or hippos. No more African sunsets. No more welcoming villagers or laughing children. They are gone, and I miss them.

I will miss Africa for years to come.

INDEX

ABOUT THE AUTHOR

Gregory Scott Kreikemeier is a young writer and professional photographer. He holds a zoology degree from the University of Georgia, where he specialized in Caribbean tropical reef systems. A dedicated conservationist, environmentalist, and naturalist, Gregory Scott is founder and president of Earth Scenes, a company committed to promoting educational awareness of the environment through specially produced posters, books, and other reference material. As part of his commitment to education, the author has lectured throughout the United States on such topics as the marine environment, nature expeditions, photography, and scuba diving.

As a science adventurer, Gregory Scott has participated in land and water expeditions around the world. While still a college student, he worked as a marine naturalist in the British Virgin Islands in an expedition sponsored by the Cousteau Society. It was at that time that he learned advanced underwater photography techniques from Jean-Michele Cousteau.

Gregory Scott lives in Georgia. He especially enjoys rock climbing and snow boarding. He is currently working on material for future Earth Scenes projects and is planning a major trans-South America expedition.